Here's Hermione

A Rosy Cole Production

by Sheila Greenwald

 Little, Brown and Company

BOSTON   TORONTO   LONDON

First Edition

The characters and events in this book are fictitious. Any similarity to real
persons, living or dead, is coincidental and not intended by the author.

Library of Congress Cataloging-in-Publication Data

Greenwald, Sheila.
  Here's Hermione : a Rosy Cole production / by Sheila Greenwald. —
1st ed.
    p.   cm.
  Summary: Rosy becomes the manager of her best friend's unusual rock
band.
  ISBN 0-316-32715-8
  [1. Musicians — Fiction. 2. Bands (Music) — Fiction.
3. Friendship — Fiction.]   I. Title.
  PZ7.G852He   1991
  [Fic] — dc20   90-24876

Joy Street Books are published by
Little, Brown and Company (Inc.)

10 9 8 7 6 5 4 3 2 1

MV

Published simultaneously in Canada
by Little, Brown & Company (Canada) Limited

Printed in the United States of America

Chapter One

My name is Hermione Wong. Remember it! One day it will be a household word. I am only eleven years old, but ever since I was ten and a half I have known I would be famous. What I haven't known is for what.

I am always thinking about what it would be like to be famous. The only time I don't think about it is when I play the cello. I love playing the cello. Other things I love are (1) listening to good cellists play the cello and (2) being with Rosy Cole, who is my best friend.

Why do I want to be famous?

I'll tell you why.

One afternoon Rosy and I were walking home from school. All of a sudden we saw a huge crowd, running and laughing and excited, rushing down Lexington Avenue toward an apartment house.

"What's up?" we asked.

"It's Pomona!" someone shrieked.

"Who's Pomona?" I asked Rosy.

"You don't know?" Rosy looked stunned. "She's world famous."

"But what's all the fuss about?"

"Haven't you seen anyone who is world famous before?" asked Rosy.

I thought I had. Once I was with my father, waiting at the deli counter for our number to be called.

"Look," my father whispered to me, and he pointed to a man with white hair who was trying to signal the deli man. "That is the world's greatest violinist."

The world's greatest violinist was saying, "I think it's my turn. I'll take three herring in cream sauce and a half-sour pickle."

If that was what being world famous meant, I couldn't see the point. But right away I knew Pomona was different. She would never have to wait her turn on the deli line.

"What does Pomona do?" I asked Rosy.

"She's a rock star." Rosy rolled her eyes. "Oh, Hermione, you don't know anything if you don't know about Pomona."

It's true. I don't know much about rock stars, but as soon as I got a look at Pomona, I knew that being a world-famous rock star was not the same as being a

world-famous violinist. In fact it wasn't the same as anything under the sun. It was as if she *was* the sun and everyone was trying to be near her to get warm and happy.

"I have a book about her," Rosy said. "Would you like to borrow it?"

"You bet I would."

That night I read all about Pomona and her backup band, the Pompoms.

The next day I went to the magazine store. It wasn't hard to find out about Pomona.

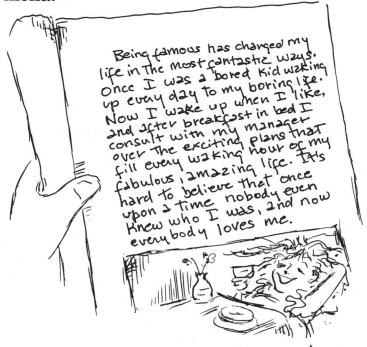

Being famous has changed my life in the most fantastic ways. Once I was a bored kid waking up every day to my boring life. Now I wake up when I like, and after breakfast in bed I consult with my manager over the exciting plans that fill every waking hour of my fabulous, amazing life. It's hard to believe that once upon a time nobody even knew who I was, and now everybody loves me.

From then on I knew I had to be famous just like Pomona. I told Rosy on the way to school, "Being famous could change my life in the most fantastic way."

"Don't be silly," Rosy said. "How would you ever do it?"

"Maybe my friend would write a book about me" — I gave Rosy a very penetrating look — "just like Pomona's friend wrote a book about her. The book could be called *Here's Hermione*. It could be made into a movie. I would write a song for the movie and call it 'Hermione, Hermione, Hermione.' Then I would sing the song, and it would be a platinum record."

"Why don't you write the book yourself?" Rosy suggested. (She's never been great at picking up hints.)

"I tried once," I said, "but I changed my mind. After all, did Alice in Wonderland have to write her own book?"

I decided it would be easier to become famous if a great movie director would notice me.

Pomona was discovered in a cafeteria, but it could happen anywhere. When I walk down the street, I pretend that a famous director is about to spot me from a passing taxicab, so I try to look my best. Just in case.

"I still don't understand why you want to be famous like Pomona." Rosy shook her head.

"Because everybody loves her, and she has a fabulous, amazing life. If I got famous all of a sudden, my whole life would change," I said. "Instead of being boring Hermione Wong, who lives on the boring Upper East Side of Manhattan and walks to boring Miss Read's School for Girls every boring morning with her best friend, who lives in the same boring building and is in the same boring class, I could be a star . . . just like Pomona."

Last month I was trying to explain this to Rosy again as she was walking me to the crosstown bus that I take to my cello lesson.

"But what kind of star would you be?" Rosy wanted to know.

"Rock stars are the biggest," I said.

"A rock star?" Rosy hooted. "A few weeks ago, you didn't even know who Pomona was."

"I've been studying up on her," I said. "Now I know a lot."

Rosy shook her head. "To be a star you can't just imitate Pomona. You have to be original and do something nobody ever did before."

"I'm racking my brains," I said. "What could it be?"

"Sometimes the answer is right in front of you," Rosy said helpfully, "something really obvious."

I looked in front of me,

 and all around me.

"That's it!" I practically screamed. "It's right here in front of me and I didn't even know it!"

"Your hand?" Rosy was puzzled.
"My cello," I said.

"Your cello?" Rosy said. "But I thought you were going to be a rock star."

"My rock cello." I held my cello up right in front of her face. Rosy can be slow to catch on.

"I've heard of soft rock and hard rock and folk rock and punk rock," Rosy said. "But I never heard of cello rock."

"Then I will be the first," I said. This was getting better and better.

"You will be the *very* first." Rosy was whispering. Even she was getting excited.

"We have to talk," I told Rosy. "This is a VITD" — our code for Very Important Thing to Discuss.

"I got on my bus, and Rosy waved to me. Anybody watching might have thought I was only going across town to my cello lesson, but I knew I was starting the most exciting journey of my life.

Chapter Two

I have to admit Tuesday and Thursday are my least boring days of the week. This is because every Tuesday and Thursday I go to Ms. Radzinoff's School of Music. On Tuesday I have a cello lesson with Ms. Radzinoff (Radzy for short), and on Thursday I play in a trio. The trio is Debbie Prusock on viola and Linda Dildine on piano, with me doing cello. Before Rosy dropped out, she played violin and we were a quartet.

Ms. Radzinoff is married to Rosy's uncle Ralph. He is a famous photographer who once wanted to write a book about Rosy playing her violin. He would have called his book *A Very Little Fid-dler*.

Now here I was taking the crosstown bus to my lesson thinking that, with a little luck, Uncle Ralph would write *Here's Hermione* and start me down my road to fame and stardom.

Right at the beginning of my lesson, Ms. Radzinoff said, "Hermione, you are playing very well. Keep it up. Remember, in only three weeks we have the annual spring recital."

Remember? Did she think I could forget?

"As I told you, a group of guest musicians and teachers will select one of my pupils to perform at our school benefit concert at Town Hall in June. The lucky winner will have the honor of performing on the same program with some of the best musicians of the day. For your solo piece I want you to play 'The Swan,' by Camille Saint-Saëns." She gave me a big smile. "If you continue to work this well, who knows? Maybe you will be chosen."

"If I am, it could be the lucky break I need to start me down my road to fame and stardom," I blurted out.

Radzy laughed. "Slow down, Hermione. Remember, all my students are talented. Hard work and fine playing are what's important. Even so, sometimes very gifted people never become famous or attract a lot of attention, while others who have a mysterious something and less talent do. My advice to you is to pay attention to your music and forget about being famous."

Forgetting about being famous was as hard as forgetting that *all* her students were talented.

After my class I waited outside the studio door to check out my competition. Betsy Linsky sounded like a squeaky shopping cart.

Charlie Dibble did a perfect imitation of chalk on a blackboard. I went home happy.

As soon as I walked in the door my mother asked me to set the table.

"Aunt Dylice and Uncle Dennis are coming for dinner with Cousin Bryan and Little Louise."

Aunt Dylice is president of her own computer company. Uncle Dennis is a physicist. Cousin Bryan's won every prize at the School for the Scientifically Gifted, and Little Louise is a genius with a super-high IQ.

When they come to dinner my mother uses the good china and almost always breaks something. After they leave she says, "Isn't it wonderful when the family gets together?" And then she bursts into tears.

In the kitchen my father was preparing his specialty, sautéed mushrooms. He gave me a big wink, as if to say, Nothing lasts forever, not even dinner with Aunt Dylice.

As soon as she came in the door, Aunt Dylice began to make announcements. "Bryan just won the All-City Science Prize," she said,

"and Little Louise is reading Latin."

"Latin?" my mother repeated, looking at me.

"I can read Latin," I joked. "L-A-T-I-N."

Nobody laughed.

Louise pulled on my arm. "Let's go to your room, Hermione. I'd like to see your books."

"I don't have any in Latin," I told her.

When Louise saw my books she began to giggle. "I don't read books like this anymore."

"Why do you save all your baby books?" Cousin Bryan asked without looking at me. He always stares over my head as if my eyes were too far beneath his to bother with.

I didn't tell him they were not my baby books.

At dinner Mom announced, "Hermione will be playing the cello in her music school's recital in three weeks. If she is selected she will perform in June at the school's benefit concert at Town Hall on the same program as some of the finest musicians in the city."

"How wonderful!" Aunt Dylice said. "I would love to be there to see my favorite little niece win such a fantastic prize."

"We would love to invite you all." Mom glanced at me as if to check. Would I win the fantastic prize?

"By the way, did I tell you Louise is translating de Maupassant short stories into Chinese?" Aunt Dylice smiled at the whole table.

Just then my mother's glass of water slipped out of her hand and broke on the tile trivet.

After our guests left, we picked up the pieces and vacuumed the carpet. Then my mother collapsed in the living room and sighed. "Isn't it wonderful when the family gets together?" she said and burst into tears. "I'm two years older than Dylice, and what have I done with my life?" she cried.

"How about me?" I asked.

"Oh, yes, you." Mom sniffled. "But I mean I'm not president of anything. I just try to help Dad get jobs designing kitch-ens."

"Wait a minute," I said. "What if I were world famous?"

"What are you talking about?" my mother asked.

"She's saying that if she were world famous, Dylice would keep quiet about Little Louise." Dad laughed.

"Oh, sure." My mother laughed, too.

I was glad I had made her laugh, but I wasn't joking. I could just imagine Aunt Dylice and Cousin Bryan and Little Louise watching while I walked off with the music-school prize. And that would be only the beginning.

Chapter Three

The next day when I got home from school, I headed over to Rosy's with my cello. "Three weeks till the recital," I told her. "That doesn't give me much time to put myself together like a rock star."

"How will you begin?" she asked.

"At the bottom," I said. "Where are those boots that don't fit you anymore?"

We found them at the back of her closet.

"The boots are an improvement," Rosy said.

"Not enough," I said.

With wooden blocks left over from a building set and a few nail studs, we created a look for the boots that took most of an hour.

"Now what?" Rosy asked me.

"I'm not sure," I said. "Maybe it's time for research." I knew Rosy knew I was not talking about going to the library.

Rosy's sisters are in high school. Pippa plays electric guitar, and Anitra plays drums and keyboard. They have a huge collection of records and posters. Even though they weren't home yet, we learned a whole lot just by being in their room. First Rosy made a list of things I could use, and then we went to search for them.

In Anitra's closet we found a leotard from the days when she studied ballet. In Pippa's corner we discovered a mike.

I put on the leotard and held the mike. Rosy squinted at me as if I were a record cover. She opened her everything drawer. "You need more hair," she said.

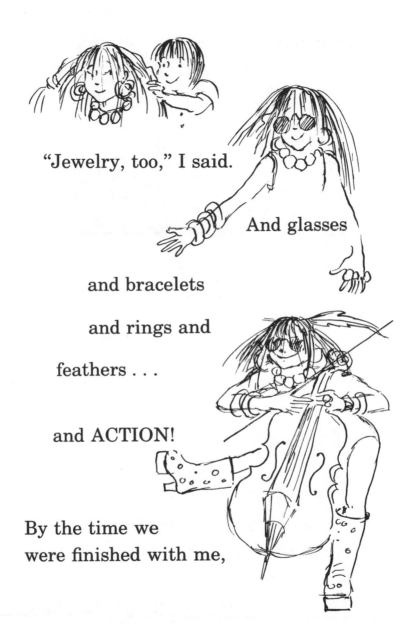

"Jewelry, too," I said.

And glasses

and bracelets

and rings and

feathers . . .

and ACTION!

By the time we
were finished with me,

I really did have a look.

Anitra and Pippa walked in.

"Hermione is trying to be a rock star," Rosy explained.

"That's obvious," Anitra said. "She

looks just like every other rock star."

"If you want to make it in rock, you've got to have a gimmick that's original," Pippa said.

"What's a gimmick?" Rosy asked.

"A trick so that people notice you," Pippa said.

"A good gimmick plus a lucky break and, who knows, you could end up like Pomona."

"That is exactly what I had in mind," I told her. It made me feel really good to know that somebody understood what I was trying to accomplish.

When I got home, my mother gasped. "Hermione, what on earth are you up to? You don't look at all like yourself."

"That's the point," I said. "How do you expect me to be a famous rock star if I look like myself?"

"We certainly don't expect you to be a famous rock star, especially if it's going to make you a famous fruitcake," my mother said.

"Once I'm a famous rock star," I told her, "I'll be on top of the world, and you can call Aunt Dylice and tell her Little Louise can translate Chop Suey into Pastrami and Cousin Bryan can win the biggest prize on earth, but Hermione is FAMOUS."

"Why don't you take a nap?" my mother suggested.

I had told my mother too much, and she didn't understand. I went to my room, but I was too upset to take a nap. After one whole afternoon, I had no gimmick, I had no look. I didn't know what to do, so I took out my cello and began to tune it. Then I opened my music and started to play "The Swan."

Soon I forgot all about Little Louise and
Cousin Bryan

and a look that was
a gimmick.

34

I forgot to worry about
being chosen to play
at the School of
Music benefit

so I could become famous.

Soon the music had made me feel a
hundred percent okay.

Chapter Four

But on the way to school the next morning, Rosy gave me some bad news. "Pippa and Anitra say that to be a rock star you have to have a band," she told me.

She was right, of course. Pomona had the Pompoms. How could I have forgotten? "But where do I find a band?" I asked Rosy.

"Maybe it's right in front of you, like your cello was," Rosy suggested.

Right in front of me, going up the steps to school, were Linda Dildine and Debbie Prusock. I looked at Rosy. "You're right," I said.

"There they are. My band."

When I told Linda and Debbie, Debbie said, "I don't get it."

"What do we play?" Linda asked.

"We could play the Bach piece we are working on at music school, plus some original works by me," I said.

"You have original works?" Debbie said. She looked really doubtful.

"I will by this afternoon when we have our first rehearsal," I said.

"This afternoon?" Linda blinked.

"Right after school, at my place," I said.

"I'll have to go home first and get my viola," Debbie said.

"Bring your boots, too," Rosy told them.

At three-thirty Rosy came over with a mike that Pippa had said we could borrow.

Debbie and Linda arrived right after Rosy. Their boots needed a lot of work.

When the boots were finally ready, Linda said to me, "If you wear a leotard, Debbie and I should wear leotards, too. Otherwise what would the audience think?"

"They would think that I need to take off ten pounds," Debbie said. "I won't wear a leotard."

"I have an idea," Rosy piped up. "Since we're going to play a little Bach, why not dress up like him?"

"Bach in boots?" Linda said.

"The Bach Rockers." Rosy snapped her fingers.

"Hermione Wong and the Bach Rockers," I corrected her.

"A Rosy Cole production," Rosy added.

"I wonder if it might even be our gimmick." I began to get excited. "This could be just what we need."

We found a picture of Bach on the front of our music.

White powder for the hair.

Bows for the ponytails.

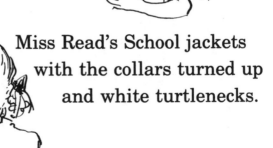

Miss Read's School jackets
with the collars turned up
and white turtlenecks.

When we sat down to play, Rosy gave us a big hand. "The Bach Rockers," she said, smiling. "It works."

It was the last thing that did.

"First we will play one of my original pieces," I told my band. I began the melody for them on my cello.

"This sounds like something you are making up on the spot," Debbie interrupted.

"It's supposed to," I said. "It's called improvisation. I have two more."

Debbie and Linda looked at each other.

"I have an improvisation, too," Debbie said. "Let's do mine."

"If you want to do your own improvisation, you should put together your own band," I said.

"You mean *you* get to pick all the pieces?" Linda chimed in.

"It's my band," I reminded her.

"I agreed to be in a band, not a dictatorship." Linda started to stand up. So did Debbie.

"Sit down," Rosy told them. "Hermione

will let you each do an improvisation of your own."

"Who says I will?" I asked Rosy.

"Your manager," Rosy snapped at me. "Otherwise there won't be any band."

Right away I could see her point. First we did Linda's improvisation.

Then we did Debbie's, and

then we did mine.

"Maybe we should call this band the Bad Sports," Rosy muttered.

"Where do we perform?" Linda asked. "When is our first gig?"

"How about the School of Music's spring concert?" I said.

Debbie looked worried. "Did you ask permission?"

"Not exactly." I looked at Rosy. "I think we should leave it as a surprise. It will be more exciting that way."

"But we can't play for the first time at the recital. We need practice in front of an audience," Linda said.

"That's right," Debbie agreed. "We should have gigs before the concert so we're really ready."

"You call yourself the manager," I said to Rosy. "Where will you book us?"

"Bring your instruments to school on Monday. I'll have a gig for you," Rosy said. She beamed her confident smile.

Just before they left, Debbie had a suggestion. "If we want to stick together, we better not rehearse anymore. Rehearsing makes us argue."

"No more rehearsals." Linda nodded. "Just gigs."

We all agreed.

Chapter Five

Monday morning I brought my cello to school. "What's the plan?" I asked Rosy.

She was carrying a piece of rolled-up oaktag. It was a leftover poster from a club we once had. I could see she'd used the other side. "I'll show you when we get to school," Rosy said.

As soon as we sat down in homeroom, Rosy opened the poster.

"What's a lunch concert?" Debbie asked.

"A concert with lunch," I guessed.

"Exactly." Rosy grinned. "Just like at Alfredo's on the Park. It's a very popular idea."

There is a piano in the lunchroom, so we were able to tune up and find out if Rosy was right.

She wasn't.

Right away, something told me my band had a problem. It wasn't just the audience response, which could have been more enthusiastic; it was something about our playing. We were each improvising all right, but we were not improvising together. Linda even started banging out her Bach solo for the recital.

Rosy kept smiling and cheering us on, and actually I thought things were looking up when some of the kitchen staff joined in, but then Mrs. Palmer, our

lunchroom teacher, called out, "I am sorry, Hermione, but I will have to ask you to stop. You cannot keep making this terrible noise."

"Terrible noise?" I was shocked.

Debbie put her viola in its case. "The Bach Rockers are history," she said and snapped the case shut.

"Now I know why people rehearse," Rosy said.

"We argue if we rehearse," I reminded her.

"And we sound awful if we don't," Debbie summed up.

"I guess you'll just have to make your mark with your solo piece," Rosy told me.

" 'The Swan,' by Camille Saint-Saëns," I said. "It doesn't sound like rock-star material to me."

"You're so good at the cello, maybe you don't need a look and a gimmick," Rosy said.

"Pomona says being good isn't enough," I explained. "Even Radzy told me that to be famous you have to have a mysterious something."

"I hope you have better luck with your mysterious something than you had with your band." Rosy sighed.

That night I decided to practice twice as hard. I thought maybe an idea would come to me. I played "The Swan" over and over.

My mother knocked on my door. "Your playing is excellent," she called, "but it's time for bed."

"Just another fifteen minutes?" I pleaded.

"It's time for bed," my mother repeated. "This recital is not the most important thing in the world."

Maybe the recital wasn't the most important thing in the world, but being famous was. When I was famous my life would be fabulous and amazing and everything I did would be great, even the Bach Rockers.

WORLD-FAMOUS HERMIONE WONG
and the
FAbulous Amazing BAch Rockers

ALL SOLD OUT

Chapter Six

A few weeks later, Ms. Radzinoff said, "One of my guests at the recital will be the world-famous cello teacher Joseph Pitkin. He is an old friend. I want him to hear you play. All my students have come a long way, but you have made really remarkable progress."

All her students? Even Betsy Linsky?

When my lesson was over, I stayed in the hallway outside the studio door so I could check out my competition.

When Betsy walked in, I didn't think I had anything to worry about.

But when I heard the sounds of the cello, I couldn't believe my ears. The music was so beautiful, Joseph Pitkin would choose her. I didn't stand a chance.

Just when I thought it couldn't get any worse, the door opened.

"Oh, Hermione." Radzy smiled. "Come on in. I'm playing Betsy a recording of Joseph Pitkin performing the piece she has been studying. You might as well listen, too."

I was so happy it wasn't Betsy Linsky,

I forgot to be embarrassed about falling
on the floor.

When I got home my mother said, "Where have you been, Hermione? Did you forget that Aunt Dylice and her family are coming for dinner?"

"Again?" I moaned.

I went straight to my room and looked at the calendar. There were only three days till the recital. Time was running out. I had to find my gimmick soon.

I opened my music and set it on the stand.

I remembered that Rosy always said sometimes the answer to a problem is right in front of you. I looked right in front of me and . . . sure enough.

It was so wonderful to have my look and a real gimmick at last that I didn't even care that Aunt Dylice and her family were ringing the doorbell. I could hardly wait for them to come (and go) so I could get to work.

"Were you practicing your cello?" Little Louise asked as soon as she saw me.

"Do you think you'll win the prize?" Cousin Bryan stared at a spot above my head.

"If she plays the best she can, that's the true prize," my father said.

"Speaking of prizes," Aunt Dylice said in her announcement voice, "Bryan has just won the Math Achievement Award."

Speaking of prizes made me think of the recital and my exciting new idea. "When I win my prize," I blurted out, "I promise you all a very big surprise."

"What surprise?" My mother looked around her as if she expected something to explode.

"Never mind." I shook my head. I had to be careful not to say too much. "You'll know soon enough."

After Aunt Dylice and her family finally went home, I hurried to my closet to check and see if I had the things I would need.

I was just getting started when my mother called in that it was time for me to go to bed. I didn't mind. Now that I knew what I was going to do, I got into bed and went right off to sleep.

The next morning on the way to school, I almost told Rosy what I was planning, but I remembered something Pomona said: "Every breakthrough idea I ever had for my career came from within myself. My managers always tried to talk me out of them. The more original, the more scared they were of my trying them."

"I can tell by your face that you're up to something," Rosy said. "Since I'm your manager, you better tell me."

"If I told you, it would ruin the surprise."

"Is it a surprise you're cooking up," Rosy asked, "or a shock?"

"A little bit of both."

When I got home from school in the afternoon, my mother showed me a new dress she had bought for me to wear to the recital.

I tried it on.

SWEET THING

"Oh, that is so sweet," my mother gushed.

I couldn't wait to take the dress off and get to work on my real recital clothes.

I used cardboard and Scotch tape and crayons and pillows, too.

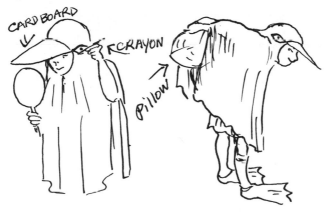

On Friday the twenty-sixth of May, I put on my new recital dress and packed a shopping bag with the clothes I would change into.

"What's in that bag?" my mother asked.

"Just accessories," I told her, pulling the bag closer.

My mother and I took a taxi across town to the School of Music.

Radzy and other teachers had opened the sliding doors on the parlor floor of the brownstone building so that it made one large space. There were flowers in big vases on either side of the piano. There were rows and rows of chairs for the audience. Rosy was there with her parents

and her uncle Ralph. Debbie's parents were there, and so were her two brothers. Linda Dildine's whole family filled the second row. My parents sat with Aunt Dylice, Cousin Bryan, and Little Louise.

I saw people I had never seen before. I wondered which of them was Joseph Pitkin.

Radzy got up and welcomed everyone. Then she introduced the intermediate string quartet. They played something by Schubert. After that each of them did a solo. Charlie Dibble lost his place and had to repeat.

Betsy Linsky played by heart and didn't make a single mistake.

Mimi Thompson's dress was so fantastic I was sure nobody would notice her wrong notes.

Soon it was time for our trio. We did the Bach. Everybody applauded and smiled and looked happy. Next Linda played her piano solo. The row of Dildines went wild.

When Debbie got up to play, her parents looked as if they'd gone to heaven.

I went to the bathroom so I could change into my accessories.

When I was ready, I opened the door to the hallway just in time to hear Radzy announcing that "Hermione Wong will now play 'The Swan' by Camille Saint-Saëns."

As I walked before the audience, there was a hush followed by a low murmuring and finally some strange choking noises. I thought I heard Rosy gasp. I was certainly getting a big reaction. It seemed to me my idea was working just the way I'd hoped it would.

I began to sit down so I could tune up.
Right away I wished I'd practiced playing in my look.

There were some problems.
For one thing, sitting down.

For another, being able to see my music
and move my head.

Then, just as I was about to play, my
bow got stuck in my wing.

In a way it didn't matter. Even if I could have freed it up to play, nobody could have heard me — they were laughing too hard. I decided the only thing I could do was get back to the bathroom . . . FAST!

Even that was a problem.

Chapter Seven

Rosy was banging on the door. "I have to talk to you." She sounded really angry.

"I can't talk," I said. "I'm busy." (I *was* busy . . . crying.)

"There's punch and cookies in the front room." Rosy sugared her voice up like the cookies, but it didn't fool me. "Fudge brownies with pecans."

"I'm not hungry."

"Just look at it this way," she said, taking a deep breath. I could almost hear her brain trying to think up a way for me to look at it. "What you did was an experiment, a piece of performance art."

"Are you kidding?"

"If you don't come out of there," Rosy snapped, "you will ruin my reputation. Please remember you are a Rosy Cole production." She was quiet for a moment. "Also, Radzy will kill you."

I opened the door a crack, and Rosy pushed her way in. "Why didn't you let me manage you?" she fumed.

"I wanted to be like Pomona," I began to blubber. "Original and unforgettable."

Rosy bent down and yanked off my flippers. "Well, you got what you wanted," she said.

I put on my recital dress and my shoes and looked around for a trapdoor. Since there wasn't one, I let Rosy pull me into the hall.

The whole audience was standing around in the room across from where the recital had been. There was a long table covered with platters of cookies and bowls of Radzy's pink punch. There were the Coles and the Prusocks and the Dildines, looking as if something wonderful had just happened.

And there were the Wongs . . . looking as if it hadn't.

"Hermione," my mother croaked. "What a surprise you gave us."

"You can say that again," Aunt Dylice said, popping a cookie in her mouth.

My father put his arm around my shoulder. "That was a very original and creative idea you had, Hermione." He smiled. "One day you will see it wasn't the end of the world."

"Not the world," I said. "Just me."

Little Louise pulled on my wrist. "I'll bet you didn't know your piece," she whispered in my ear. "So you put on crazy clothes and made a show instead. I do that when I'm not prepared."

"I *was* prepared," I told her. I could tell that Little Louise was trying to be nice for once. I could also tell that if she knew so much about faking it, she was probably no genius.

Cousin Bryan wasn't looking over my head; he was just pretending I didn't exist. I couldn't blame him. I wished I could do the same.

"Why didn't you tell me what you were planning — " my mother began, but Radzy tapped her glass. Everyone stopped talking.

"I have an exciting announcement," she said. "Our panel of judges has made a difficult decision. Out of the many fine young artists you just heard, they have selected the one who will perform at our benefit concert at Town Hall in June." She cleared her throat to prolong the suspense. You could have heard the ice melting in the punch bowls.

"Linda Dildine," Radzy said.

Right away, the Dildines went into orbit, except for Linda, who looked a little bit sick.

"Me?" she finally squeaked.

"There's another Linda Dildine?" Rosy rolled her eyes.

Radzy shook Linda's hand and presented her with a little bunch of flowers. Rosy's uncle Ralph took her picture.

I wanted to lie down on the floor like the carpet. Everybody began to clap and smile at Linda and say, "Isn't she adorable?" and Uncle Ralph *took another picture* of her. . . . I could just imagine where this would end up: *Here's Dildine* or *A Very Little Piano Player*.

It was too much. I couldn't stand another minute. When no one was looking, I quietly walked across the hall into the concert room. My cello was just where I had left it, as always, waiting for me whenever I needed it.

I closed my eyes and began to play "The Swan." I had been practicing it for weeks. As soon as I began the first notes, I felt better. The music filled my head until there was no more room for feeling miserable or mixed up.

The music didn't know about a look or a gimmick. It didn't know about getting noticed or being a famous star.

When I finished my piece and opened my eyes, I couldn't believe them.

Little Louise was standing right in front of me. "You really were prepared! Oh, Hermione, that was wonderful!"

Aunt Dylice leaned down and gave me a hug. My parents were both smiling.

Even Cousin Bryan was looking right at me and grinning. Others who had drifted across the hall when they heard the music began to applaud.

I hadn't been selected by the judges and I might not be on my road to fame and stardom, but at least the day hadn't been a total disaster.

Chapter Eight

Even if the day of the recital hadn't been a total disaster, Saturday morning was. I woke up in the middle of a terrible dream. My dream was that I walked into a room and Joseph Pitkin and Ms. Radzinoff were standing in the middle of it, looking very sad.

My mother came in with a cup of tea and some slices of toast on a tray. "Hermione, are you sick?"

I rolled over and faced the wall. "I don't want to see anyone."

She sat on the end of my bed. "Perhaps there is a lesson in all this," she said.

There had already been a bad dream. Did there have to be a lesson, too?

I sat up in bed and saw my cello on its stand near the corner. I was ashamed to even look at it.

I was just beginning to sip my tea when the phone rang. It was Rosy.

"I've decided to forgive what you did yesterday," she said.

"So?"

"So my parents are having a brunch. They asked me to pick up the food order at Gourmet-Take-Away. I can't manage it alone."

"I'm under the weather," I said.

"Goofing up at a recital is not a disease," Rosy snapped. "Meet me in the lobby by the elevator in twenty minutes."

Sure enough, twenty minutes later Rosy was standing next to the elevator with a shopping cart. "We're having Radzy and Uncle Ralph," she chirped, "and some other people, too." She gave me her sideways look as if I should be just dying to know who the other people would be.

On the way to the store, we passed a

sign in front of the Y on Ninety-Second
Street.

"Remember him?" Rosy had a sly look.

"How could I forget?"

Waiting on line at the Gourmet-Take-Away was Linda Dildine's grandmother.

"Aren't you the little girl who played the cello yesterday?" She looked me up and down as if I were one of the cheeses hanging from the ceiling.

"Yes, she is," Rosy the mouthpiece answered. "Wasn't she great?"

"We couldn't get over it," the woman said.

That made two of us.

Rosy picked up her mother's order and loaded it into the shopping cart. I carried the bag full of different breads that didn't fit.

When we got out of the elevator on Rosy's floor, we could hear voices and laughter coming from her apartment. Just as Rosy put her key in the lock, it got quiet. Suddenly there was a new sound altogether, the most beautiful sound I had ever heard. We stood outside the door and listened.

When it was over, we tiptoed into Rosy's foyer and looked down the hall into her living room.

It was my bad dream come true.

Sitting there were Rosy's parents and her sisters and Radzy and Uncle Ralph and . . . Joseph Pitkin.

I started to back out the door, but Radzy saw me. "Hermione Wong," she boomed. "Did Rosy tell you?"

Everyone turned to stare at me.

"Tell me what?"

"Joseph Pitkin has agreed to give you lessons."

Joseph Pitkin stood up and stared at me, a deep serious stare.

"He only takes a few students," Radzy said, beaming.

"You are good, Hermione." Mr Pitkin nodded. "With a lot of hard work, dedication, discipline, and some sacrifice, you could be very good."

"Very good?" I repeated. "As good as you?" I squeaked.

He smiled. "With hard work and discipline and a love for the music, who knows?"

For a minute everyone was quiet. Then Rosy's father took my hand and shook it. "Congratulations, Hermione," he said.

"Now it's time to celebrate," Rosy's mother said. She began to pass around glasses of spicy tomato juice.

"I have to go home now," I told Mrs. Cole. "There's something I forgot to do."

Rosy looked surprised. "Can't it wait?" she asked suspiciously.

"It can't." I shook my head.

"Are you feeling all right?" Rosy followed me to the door.

"Never better," I said, and I rang for the elevator. "That's why I have to go home now."

Rosy shook her head. "Sometimes I don't understand you at all, Hermione Wong," she said.

How could I explain
that I felt so good
there was only one
thing I wanted to do?
I wanted to do it
more than I wanted
to be at a party,
more even than I wanted
to be a famous rock star like Pomona. I
could hardly wait.

It was something that made me feel warm
and happy and full
of light like the sun. . . .

It really had been there all the time.